JEMIMA PUDDLE-DUCK'S HILLTOP FARM

MR. MCGREGOR'S GARDEN

MR. TOD & TOMMY BROCK'S WOOD

MY BURROW

DR. & MRS. BOBTAIL'S BURROW (LILY'S HOME)

TUNNEL NETWORK

MR. BOUNCER'S BURROW (BENJAMIN'S HOME)

RAVINE

DEEP DARK WOODS

My friend, **Lily Bobtail**. Whatever the problem, she's got the answer.

Benjamin Bunny is my cousin. Wherever we go, he's right behind me—usually hiding!

It was a warm autumn morning, and Peter, Lily, and Benjamin were very excited.

"Hooray! It's Pumpkin Day!" cheered Benjamin.

A table outside Peter's burrow was piled high with tasty goodies, but something was missing . . .

"Where's the pumpkin?" said Lily.

THE GIANT

KIN

PUFFIN

Map of My Woods

This is a map of the woods where I live. You can see who else lives here, too. It's in my dad's journal, which I always have with me.

ROCKY ISLAND

OLD BROWN'S ISLAND

This is **Mr. Tod.** Foxes eat rabbits. Need I say more?

MR. JEREMY FISHER'S POND

SQUIRREL NUTKIN'S WOOD

MRS. TIGGY-WINKLE'S LAUNDRY

My mum—**Mrs. Rabbit** to you! She's definitely the best mum ever!

Cotton-tail is my littlest sister and the cheekiest.

"Don't worry," replied Peter. "I know just where to find one. Let's hop to it!"

Peter's little sister, Cotton-tail,
followed the friends all the way
to Mr. McGregor's garden.

There was the perfect
pumpkin! But the farmer's
cat was snoozing beside it.

"Quietly!" whispered Peter as the friends pushed and pulled the giant pumpkin. But try as they might, they couldn't make it budge.

Peter scratched his head.
"Lily, have you got
any rope?" he asked.

Lily reached into her
Just-in-Case Pocket.
"Let me see," she said.

"Feather . . . no.
Ah, here it is."

Peter tied one end of the rope around the pumpkin
and the other around the sleeping cat.

"Careful, Peter," said Benjamin, trembling.

Peter blew a
loud raspberry.

The cat woke
up and lunged
wildly at Peter.

"MEEEOOOW!"

"PUSH!"

Peter yelled to his friends as the angry animal strained against the rope.

Suddenly, the rope snapped! The cat tumbled forward, past the bunnies, and dashed into the house.

"What's got into you?" Mr. McGregor asked as the cat scrambled past him.

The bunnies hid
as Mr. McGregor picked
up their perfect pumpkin and
carried it to the garden table.

"He's cutting it up!"

Peter gasped.

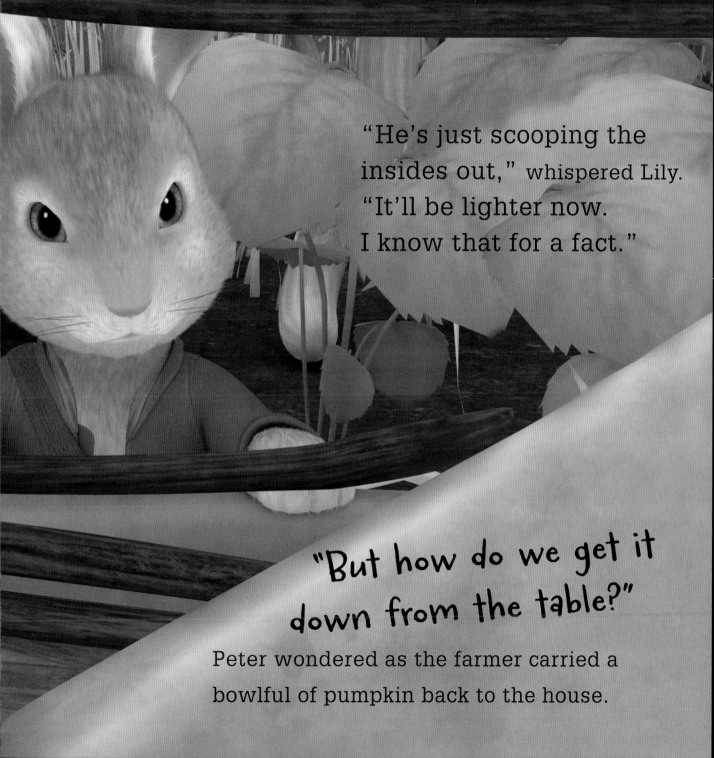

"He's just scooping the insides out," whispered Lily. "It'll be lighter now. I know that for a fact."

"But how do we get it down from the table?" Peter wondered as the farmer carried a bowlful of pumpkin back to the house.

Then the pumpkin
began to wobble and . . .

BUMP! It fell from the
table and began to roll.

Peter, Benjamin, and Lily heard a
familiar giggle coming from inside.

"Cotton-tail!" they cried, chasing after the pumpkin.

The friends jumped aboard the speeding pumpkin as it bowled down the garden path and out of the gate.

The pumpkin rolled faster and faster. As it reached the woods, it hit a bump and Peter and Lily were bounced out, leaving Cotton-tail and Benjamin spinning helplessly inside.

"It's never going to stop!"

Lily gasped, watching it roll away.

"A good rabbit
never gives up,"
Peter reminded her.
"Do you have any
more rope?"

Peter and Lily
dashed ahead. Lily
tied a line of rope
between two trees.
As the pumpkin hit
the rope, it slowed
right down and
stopped at last.

Peter and Lily
jumped inside.

"Now, let's roll this pumpkin right back to the burrow!" cried Peter.

"Everyone, push!"

But the pumpkin didn't move . . .

As Peter stuck his head out to see what was wrong, he came face-to-face with . . . Mr. Tod!

"Rabbit and pumpkin pie for dinner," laughed the fox. **"MY FAVOURITE."**

"This is bad. This is very bad," said Benjamin.

"Lily, do you still have that feather?" whispered Peter.

Lily pulled the feather from her pocket and handed it to Peter.

Peter tickled the fox's nose.

"Aah . . . aah . . . aah! CHOO!"

Mr. Tod sneezed, losing his grip and catapulting the pumpkin back through the woods towards Peter's burrow.

"Woo-hoo!
Yeah!"

whooped the bunnies excitedly
as they zoomed along.

As the speeding pumpkin approached Peter's burrow, it promptly crashed to a halt, and the bunnies all tumbled out.

"What's all this commotion?"

asked Mrs. Rabbit, appearing from the burrow.

"We're sorry," Benjamin replied. "Our pumpkin didn't have any brakes!"

"What a perfect pumpkin!" exclaimed Peter's mum, laughing. "And just in time for our Pumpkin Day party."

As family and friends ate a delicious autumn
feast, Peter grinned at Benjamin and Lily.

"Next year we'll get a **REALLY** big one!"

ON THE MOVE!

Using the cat to move the pumpkin was a brilliant plan. (It's a shame it didn't work!) Here are some more ways to move a heavy pumpkin.

Winch—to lift it over large objects

GIANT pumpkin

PULL rope

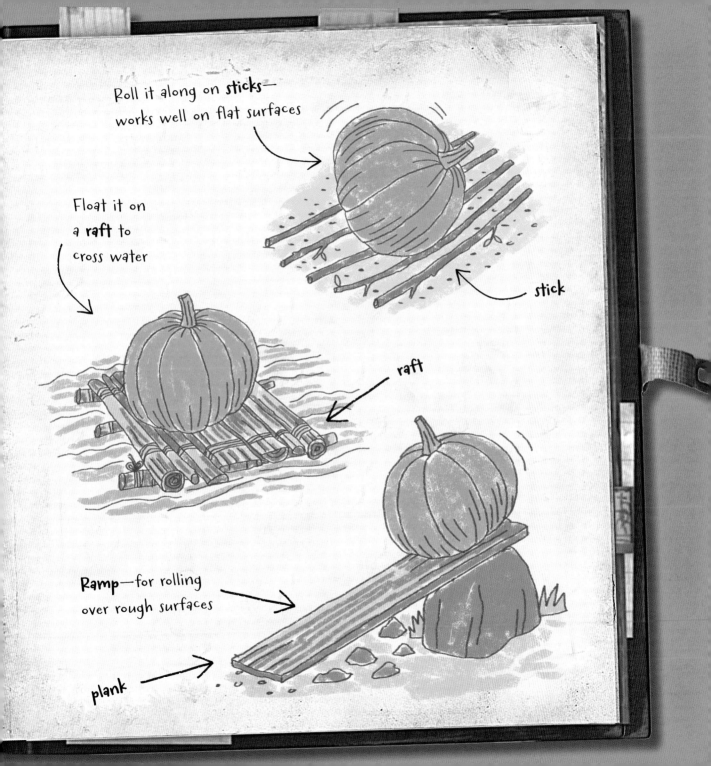

Roll it along on **sticks**—works well on flat surfaces

stick

Float it on a **raft** to cross water

raft

Ramp—for rolling over rough surfaces

plank

PUMPKIN Party Time

Peter, Lily, Benjamin, and Cotton-tail had so much fun rolling the giant pumpkin home for Pumpkin Day. Even though they didn't know how to stop it!

Ask an adult to help you make a Pumpkin Day lantern. You don't have to use a GIANT pumpkin –but big ones are best!

 Scoop out the flesh of the pumpkin.

 Draw a funny face on the outside.

 Cut out the face.

 Put a candle inside.

Use your lantern to light up your own Pumpkin Day party!

CONGRATULATIONS!

SKILL IN **LANTERN-MAKING** CERTIFICATE

Awarded to

- -

Age

- -

Peter Rabbit
- - - - - - - - - - - - - - - - -
PETER RABBIT
BEST LANTERN-MAKER IN THE WOODS

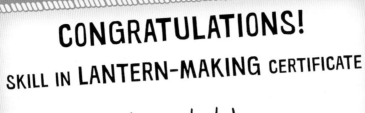

CRAFT

Happy
Pumpkin Day!